DAVID'S SEARCH

DAVID'S SEARCH

Joan Lowery Nixon

A YEARLING BOOK

To Arthur F. Smith, an orphan train rider,
who is working to establish the history of the orphan trains
in our country's history books

Published by
Dell Yearling
an imprint of
Random House Children's Books
a division of Random House, Inc.
1540 Broadway
New York, New York 10036

ISBN 0-440-41315-X

Reprinted by arrangement with Delacorte Press

Printed in the United States of America

June 2000

10 9 8 7 6 5 4 3 2 1

CWO

A Note from the Author

In the 1850s there were many homeless children in New York City. The Children's Aid Society, which was founded by Charles Loring Brace, tried to help these children by giving them new homes. They were sent west and placed with families who lived on farms and in small towns throughout the United States. From 1854 to 1929, groups of homeless children traveled on trains that were soon nicknamed orphan trains. The children were called orphan train riders.

The characters in these stories are fictional, but their problems and joys, their worries and fears, and their desire to love and be loved were experienced by the real orphan train riders of many years ago.

Joan Lowery Nixon

More orphan train stories by
Joan Lowery Nixon

The Orphan Train Adventures

A FAMILY APART
Winner of the Golden Spur Award
CAUGHT IN THE ACT
IN THE FACE OF DANGER
Winner of the Golden Spur Award
A PLACE TO BELONG
A DANGEROUS PROMISE
KEEPING SECRETS
CIRCLE OF LOVE

ORPHAN TRAIN CHILDREN

LUCY'S WISH
WILL'S CHOICE
AGGIE'S HOME

Homes Wanted
For Children

A Company of Orphan Children

of different ages in charge of an agent will arrive at your town on date herein mentioned. The object of the coming of these children is to find homes in your midst, especially among farmers, where they may enjoy a happy and wholesome family life, where kind care, good example and moral training will fit them for a life of self-support and usefulness. They come under the auspices of the New York Children's Aid Society. They have been tested and found to be well-meaning boys and girls anxious for homes.

The conditions are that these children shall be properly clothed, treated as members of the family, given proper school advantages and remain in the family until they are eighteen years of age. At the expiration of the time specified it is hoped that arrangements can be made whereby they may be able to remain in the family indefinitely. The Society retains the right to remove a child at any time for just cause, and agrees to remove any found unsatisfactory after being notified.

Remember the time and place. All are invited. Come out and hear the address. Applications may be made to any one of the following well known citizens, who have agreed to act as local committee to aid the agent in securing homes.

A. J. Hammond, H. W. Parker, Geo. Baxter, J. F. Damon, J. P. Humes, H. N. Welch, J. A. Armstrong, F. L. Durgin.

This distribution of Children is by Consent of the State Board of Control, and will take place at the

G. A. R. Hall, Winnebago, Minn.

Friday, Jan. 11th, '07, at 10.30 a. m. @ 2 p. m.

H. D. Clarke, State Agent,
Dodge Center, Minn.

Office: 105 East 22nd St.,
New York City.

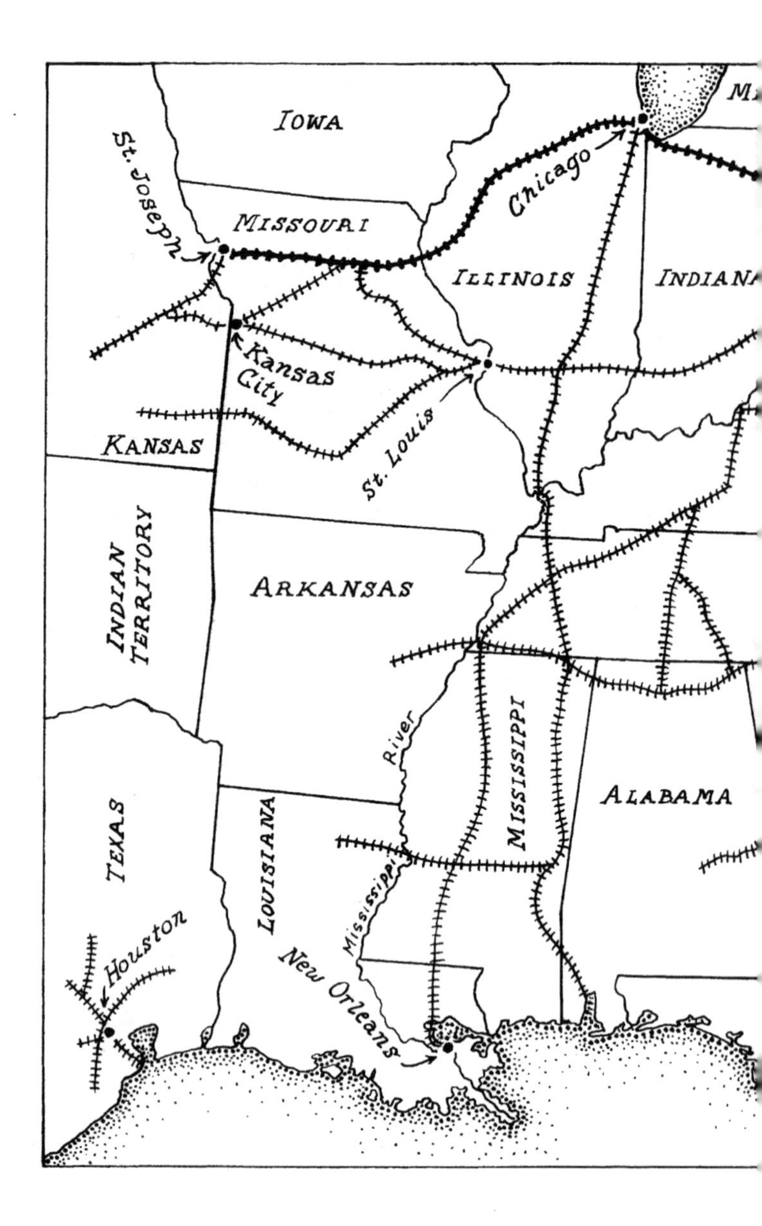

IOWA
St. Joseph
MISSOURI
Chicago
ILLINOIS
Kansas City
KANSAS
St. Louis
INDIAN TERRITORY
ARKANSAS
River
MISSISSIPPI
ALABAMA
TEXAS
LOUISIANA
Mississippi
Houston
New Orleans

Orphan Train Routes
CIRCA 1866
GAN
NEW YORK
PENNSYLVANIA
CONNECTICUT
OHIO
Pittsburgh
Philadelphia
Columbus
NEW JERSEY
New York City
Washington, D.C.
DELAWARE
KENTUCKY
WEST VIRGINIA
MARYLAND
VIRGINIA
TENNESSEE
NORTH
CAROLINA
SOUTH CAROLINA
Atlanta
GEORGIA
FLORIDA

David's Search

From the journal of
FRANCES MARY KELLY, JULY 1866

I wish I could really know and understand each of the orphan train riders in my care. I've grown close to the outgoing, talkative children and to those who are quick to tell me their needs. But some of the children are shy. They slip into the shadows of the more demanding children. With thirty children to tend to, the quiet ones are easy to overlook.

Like David Howard.

Before we left the Children's Aid Society offices to travel to Missouri, Miss Hunter told me about David, a small, thin child with brown hair.

"David's eleven and a likable, agreeable boy. He's used to doing what others tell him to. David lived on the streets until another boy brought him to us."

I was surprised. I knew how hard living on the streets could be. "David had no parents? No home? But he seems like a gentle boy—not a street fighter."

Miss Hunter nodded and said, "I know. It's amazing that he survived as long as he did."

This afternoon I settled onto the bench next to David. He was doing his best to keep from crying. "Want to tell me about it, David?" I asked.

"I miss my chum, Mickey," David answered. "He's the best chum anybody could ever have. He's a street arab and smart as—"

I couldn't help interrupting. "What did you call him?"

"A street arab," David said. "Mickey sells newspapers and shines shoes. He took care of me. He said I'd never be anything more than a guttersnipe, and not a very good guttersnipe at that."

I hurried to say, "Oh, David, I'm sure Mickey didn't mean it."

"He meant it, miss," David said. "Guttersnipes aren't clever enough to be street arabs. I tried, but I couldn't take care of myself. So Mickey said I should go west on an orphan train and find a family to take care of me."

I smiled encouragingly and said, "You'll find another friend as fine as Mickey when you go west,

David. And no matter how far apart you are, Mickey's heart will always be with you."

David smiled at me then, for the first time. He deserves a loving family, and I will see that he gets one.

Chapter One

David Howard curled up against a brick wall in the alley and tugged his ragged coat around him. "I'm cold," he said.

Mickey rolled onto his back next to David and smiled. Mickey was two years older, and taller and stronger than David. "You can't be cold," Mickey said. "Summer's almost here."

"But I *am* cold," David insisted.

"We need to feed you more," Mickey told him. He squeezed David's arm. "Look at that. You're too skinny. That's why you're cold."

David shivered, and Mickey said, "Look up, David. Look up at the stars, and you'll forget about bein' cold. Just think how lucky we are that we can sleep outside where we can see the stars."

David always did what Mickey told him to. He turned onto his back and peered upward, squinting hard. But the faraway sky was only a blur of dark and light.

As David thought about the warm days of summer he relaxed, closing his eyes. As always, Mickey was right.

David was almost asleep when Mickey's voice startled him.

"Take it from me, chum," Mickey said. "You'll never be a street arab. You're not quick. You're not tough. You're not a fighter. Besides, you're already eleven years old or thereabouts. You're too old to be nothin' but a guttersnipe with a street arab on hand to take care of you. You've gotta be a street arab yourself, or—"

"Or what?" David interrupted.

"Or get parents to take care of you."

"I had parents once," David said. "My father worked at the docks. I didn't see him much. One day he didn't come home at all. No one ever told me what happened to him."

"Maybe no one knew," Mickey said.

David nodded. "Sometimes I dream that a long time ago a woman held me and sang to me. I dream that she was my mother and she loved me."

"I'm not talkin' about dreams," Mickey said. "I'm talkin' about what's real, and that's gettin' you some new parents."

David sat up. "New parents? What are you talking about?"

"There's a place I heard about that's right here in New York City," Mickey said. "It's called the Children's Aid Society. They send homeless children to towns in the West where people take them into their own homes and be their parents."

David's heart began to pound. He grabbed Mickey's arm and asked, "What you're telling me—this is true? Really, honest true?"

Mickey sat up and grinned. He tousled David's hair. " 'Course it's true," he said. "I wouldn't lie to you."

"That means you and me, we'd live in a house, and we'd sit at a table when we ate, like the rich people in the houses uptown. We could—"

"Don't keep talkin' about *we,*" Mickey said. "It's you that's goin', not me."

In shock, David stared at Mickey. "Why aren't you going too?"

Mickey shook his head. "You ought to know the answer without my tellin' you. I know you can read 'cause I taught you myself. Don't you read any of the newspapers I sell?"

"I do, sometimes," David mumbled. He didn't want to tell his friend that it was hard to see the words unless he held the paper close to his eyes. Mickey didn't do this when he read, and David guessed he just needed practice. Maybe if he read more . . .

"Wait a minute," David said. "What does reading have to do with your not wanting to go west?"

"You know that the Civil War ended last year when the Rebs surrendered," Mickey answered.

"Yes."

"You know what the war was all about?"

David sighed. Each day he woke up wondering if he and Mickey would get enough food to fill their stomachs. Or if they'd get caught when they helped themselves to a couple of bananas or apples from a cart. Or if they'd be able to sleep through the night without being awakened and chased away by a policeman. David had had no time to think about such things as war.

But Mickey was waiting for an answer, so David said, "The war had something to do with slavery, didn't it?"

"You're partly right," Mickey told him. "At first the war was fought to keep the Southern states from leavin' and startin' their own country. But around the middle of the war President Lincoln signed some papers that put an end to slavery."

David frowned. "I still don't know what all that has got to do with going west. The war's over, isn't it?"

"Just 'cause someone says, 'Stop fightin',' it doesn't mean everybody's gonna stop," Mickey said. "In Texas, the Rebs won't give up, so they're still fightin' the war. And in Tennessee some Rebs started a society for people on the side of the South. It's called the Ku Klux Klan. And it's spreadin' all over the South and west to Texas."

"A society?" David was puzzled. "You mean like the Aces High Society over on Forty-eighth Street where the men play cards?"

"That may be the kind of society the Ku Klux Klan pretends it is," Mickey said. "But it isn't. The Klan's a *secret* society. It's for people who hate. The people in it have burned houses and killed people—people with dark skin." His voice dropped. "Like mine."

David was puzzled. What did it matter what color skin people had? Mickey was his best friend, and David never thought about the color of Mickey's skin. Try as he might, David couldn't imagine how anybody could hate enough to hurt and kill.

"The Ku Klux Klan won't dare to come to a big city like New York, so this is where I'm stayin'," Mickey said. For a moment he looked at David as if he were studying him. "For you it's different,"

Mickey added. "You're white. The Klan won't bother you. The best thing that could happen to you is to be sent to a new home in the West."

David's heart gave a lurch. "Not without you."

Mickey put an arm around David's shoulders. "Look, chum, haven't I always known what was best for you? Haven't you always done what I told you to?"

Tears burned David's eyes, but he managed to answer. "Yes."

"Going west with the other orphans is right for you, David," Mickey said quietly. "Tomorrow I'm takin' you to the Children's Aid Society. They'll clean you up and give you new clothes and send you on the train to find a new family." Mickey lay back and turned away from David. "Everything is going to be all right."

"Promise?"

"Promise."

David slowly settled back and let the tears come. He didn't want to leave Mickey. He was the only real family David had ever known. But Mickey had said that somewhere out there were a mother and father just for David. A mother and father who'd be there to hold him and love him.

Hugging the promise to himself, David drifted off to sleep.

Chapter Two

Mickey brought David to the Children's Aid Society the very next day, as he'd promised. David dreaded saying good-bye. But Mickey just shoved his hands in his pockets, gruffly said, "Good luck, chum," and turned and walked away. Now David was on his own.

Some of the boys David met at the Children's Aid Society had come from the streets, just as he had. They talked about going west to Missouri. They bragged about what they would do if the train was attacked by Indians. They kept bragging even after Miss Hunter heard them and explained they wouldn't be going far enough west to be caught up in Indian wars.

David liked Miss Hunter, who was gentle and kind. He relaxed, trusting that what she told them was true.

But sometimes the boys' voices softened and even trembled as they spoke about the people who might adopt them. David was glad to learn that he wasn't the only one who was scared.

"I don't know what it'll be like, livin' on a farm," Eddie Marsh said.

"One thing for sure, there'll be lots of animals to take care of," said Marcus Melo, who was taller than the other boys.

"What kind of animals?" David asked.

Marcus shrugged. "You know . . . horses, cows, pigs, chickens."

"There'll be cows?" David asked. "I've never seen a cow."

Marcus hooted. "Ha! He's never seen a cow."

"Have *you*?" David asked.

"Maybe. Maybe not." Marcus shrugged. "It's my own business."

"You haven't," Eddie said.

Marcus bristled. "Yeah? Well, I saw a picture of a cow once. And I know that cows give milk."

"How do they do that?" David asked.

For a moment there was silence. Then Marcus said, "You'll find that out when we get to Missouri. No need for me to tell you now."

Grinning, Eddie elbowed David. "Marcus doesn't know, either," he said.

Miss Kelly, who had been hired to care for the children on their trip west, joined them. "When I was sent to Missouri I learned how to milk a cow," she said. "And how to feed and groom the horses and work in the fields."

David liked Miss Kelly's smile, and he liked listening to her tell them what farm chores would be like. Mickey was probably right. Going west to find a new home would be a good thing to do.

A week later, the orphan train headed for Missouri. It left the city behind and moved into the countryside, where open fields were dotted with farmhouses.

Marcus jumped up from his seat to stare out a window. "Look, lads! There's a cow!" he cried out.

David squirmed in among the other boys, trying to get a place near the windows.

"That's not a cow. That's a pig," Samuel Meyer said.

"It's a cow! Pigs are shorter, with wide, fat noses."

David squinted, but he couldn't see the nose on the white-and-brown blur in the distance.

"Miss Kelly? Is that a cow or a pig?" one of the girls shouted.

Miss Kelly looked over the heads of the children who stood plastered against the windows. "It's a cow," she said.

So that's a cow, David thought. It looked harmless.

Leaning back in his seat, David wished he could share all this with Mickey. He pictured Mickey's broad smile. Mickey was David's best friend, but David knew he'd never see Mickey again.

David was traveling to a new life in a new land, and he had no idea how his future would turn out.

But he was sure that everything was going to be all right, once he found his new family. Hadn't Mickey said so?

Before the train arrived in Harwood, Missouri, the train's first stop, faces were washed, hair was combed, and jackets were brushed. David and the other boys squirmed as Miss Kelly fussed over the girls and their silly hairbows.

Finally Miss Kelly told all the children exactly what they would do. They'd march down the street to the Methodist church, where people would be waiting to meet them.

"You're fine children, and I'm proud of you," Miss Kelly said.

But David was scared, right down to his toes, which wiggled inside the too-big, almost-new shoes he'd been given. Would he find a family to care for him? Would his new parents be good to him?

And what if nobody wanted him?

Chapter Three

David tried not to move as he sat on the stage. Miss Kelly had told everyone to sit still and smile at the people who had come to see them. But David couldn't smile. The blur of faces before him was frightening. He felt like a shiny, wet fish in the market, waiting to be chosen for someone's dinner.

David perched uncomfortably on his stool until the introductions were over and people were invited to come to the stage to talk to the children.

Four men climbed onto the stage and hurried to where some of the older, bigger boys were seated. A short, stocky man huffed and puffed as he followed them, but he couldn't catch up. He stopped in front of David and frowned.

The man had a bristly gray-streaked beard and a broad belly that tightly stretched the cloth of his jacket. David was sure the buttons would pop at any minute.

"I'm Elmer Bauer," the man said without smiling. "My wife and I came to choose a boy to live with us."

David didn't know what to say. Was Mr. Bauer inviting him to go with them?

"Miss Kelly told us that you're eleven," Mr. Bauer said. "You're small for your age. And you're thin." Mr. Bauer glanced at the larger boys, who were all being chosen, and shrugged. "I have an important question for you. Are you in good health?"

"Yes," David answered.

"Are your teeth in good condition? Open your mouth and show me."

Surprised, David did as he was told.

Mr. Bauer nodded and grunted with satisfaction.

"Boys are like pups," he said. "You can tell by their feet if they will be big men or not. Even though you are small for your age, you have big feet, so you will grow."

David wondered if he should tell Mr. Bauer the truth about his too-large shoes. Then he saw Marcus and Sam leave the stage. They had already found new parents. Some of the other children had also been chosen. David took a couple of short breaths, trying to calm his fears. He decided he'd better not say anything about his shoes.

Mr. Bauer turned and beckoned to a pale-haired woman who stood near the stage. "Come here, Sophie," he ordered.

David decided that the woman was Mr. Bauer's wife. David smiled at Mrs. Bauer, but she didn't smile back.

"This boy will do, Sophie," Mr. Bauer said.

"He's small," Mrs. Bauer complained as she looked David up and down. "Will he be able to carry his weight?"

David didn't understand what she meant. "My chum Mickey said if I eat more I won't be so thin," he told her.

Mrs. Bauer scowled. "If we take you, you will eat your share and no more."

David stole a quick glance at Mr. Bauer's big stomach. Mrs. Bauer looked strong and sturdy too. He wasn't likely to go hungry.

"I am a fair man," Mr. Bauer told David. "You will have a room of your own with a bed and three meals a day. In exchange I will expect your help with the farm chores."

David nodded. "Miss Kelly told us about the kind of work that's done on a farm. She said we'd be expected to help. That's fine with me. I want to help."

"Very good," Mr. Bauer said. "Come with me. I will sign the papers."

David looked at Mrs. Bauer. He expected her either to agree or not agree, but she didn't say anything. David wondered if Mr. Bauer made all the decisions. David was used to doing what he was told. Maybe Mrs. Bauer was, too.

Nervously David followed the Bauers to Miss Kelly. Mr. Bauer introduced his wife and himself.

Miss Kelly smiled, but the Bauers didn't smile back. David was puzzled. He didn't know much about what parents were like. But shouldn't they look happy and smile once in a while?

Mr. Bauer stood as tall as he could and puffed out his chest. He reminded David of the pigeons that strutted around the streets of New York City.

"The committee will tell you I am a man of property, influence, and good standing in the community," Mr. Bauer boomed. "My wife and I have no children. We have thought carefully about taking in an orphan boy since we first saw the Children's Aid Society advertisement. Now we have decided. We want to take David Howard."

"You know the rules," Miss Kelly said. "David must be sent to school until he is fourteen. He must be taken to church. He must—"

Mr. Bauer waved a hand as though he were brushing away flies. "Rules. Of course there are rules. You went over them very carefully, Miss Kelly. So did the committee chairman before you arrived."

Miss Kelly studied Mr. and Mrs. Bauer. "We

want all our children to have happy homes," she said. "In six months a scout—Andrew MacNair—will visit you to see if all is well with both you and David."

Mr. Bauer huffed, "He will find nothing wrong. David will be treated well. I am a man of position and honor. Ask the committee. They will vouch for us."

"Please excuse me for a few moments. I'd like to speak with David," Miss Kelly said.

She drew David aside so that the Bauers couldn't hear them. "Mr. Bauer is right about one thing," she told David. "He *is* a man of influence and good standing in the community. But one of the committee members told me that Mr. Bauer is also known for being miserly."

"I know what being miserly means," David said. "He keeps watch over his money. Mickey and me—we never had more than a few coppers at a time, so we kept watch over our money, too."

Miss Kelly hesitated. "I want you to have a happy home, David," she said.

David shrugged. "I'll have what Mickey said I'd

have. I'll have parents to take care of me, and a real bed of my own, and enough food to fill my belly. Everything will turn out all right. Mickey said it would."

Miss Kelly put her hands on David's shoulders and looked deeply into his eyes. "Do you see the man in the black coat seated behind the table?"

David squinted. He could barely make out the man's features. "Yes," he said.

"That's Judge Winters. He's on the committee. If you need help, go to the courthouse and find him. He'll help you." Miss Kelly handed David a piece of paper. "Here's my address," she said. "You can also get in touch with me. Please write to me, David."

David looked down at his feet. Why did people want to read and write when it was so hard to make out the letters? "I'm not much of a one for reading or writing," he began. Then he stopped and smiled up at Miss Kelly. She had been kind, the way his mother must have been. David didn't want to disappoint her. "But I will write a letter to you," he added.

Miss Kelly nodded. "I hope the Bauers make you happy, David."

David knew he didn't have much of a choice. There'd been no one besides the Bauers who'd wanted to take him. He'd come with nothing. Anything that was given to him would be better than what he'd had.

That sounded like something Mickey would say, David thought, and his throat tightened. *Oh, Mickey,* he mourned, *how I wish you were here.*

Chapter Four

David sat in the back of the Bauers' wagon, holding on tightly as it bumped over the ruts in the road. It was hard to answer the Bauers' questions.

"How did you happen to be sent to Missouri?" Mrs. Bauer asked him.

"I wasn't exactly sent," David said. "My friend Mickey told me to come west. Mickey's a lot bigger than me. And he's strong and smart."

Mr. Bauer grumbled, "I'm sure *he* was one of the first to be chosen." He shook his head. "If we'd started out a few minutes earlier . . ."

"Don't blame me," Mrs. Bauer snapped. "You

should have been quicker climbing up on that stage."

David squirmed. He didn't want the Bauers to argue. He decided to tell them more about Mickey. "Mickey didn't come west. He couldn't, because of a secret society called the Ku Klux Klan."

Mrs. Bauer sniffed. "That's foolish talk," she said. "What would the Ku Klux Klan have to do with a street urchin?"

Street urchin? What was a street urchin? David would have liked to ask, but Mrs. Bauer didn't look as if she'd enjoy answering questions. "Mickey said he didn't want to go anywhere the Klan might be because people with dark skin wouldn't be safe."

"Your friend has dark skin?" Mr. Bauer said. "Then it's best he stay where he is."

"Why? I haven't heard of any Klan members around here," Mrs. Bauer argued.

"There have been rumors," Mr. Bauer said. "But who knows? Some good may come from the Klan."

David was shocked. "Good? It can't be! Mickey said the Klan hates people and kills them and burns their houses!"

"Idle talk," Mr. Bauer said. "Foolish rumors started by those who want to tarnish a group of men who are helping to rebuild our country."

"But—"

Mrs. Bauer twisted in her seat to glare at David. "One thing we need to get straight right from the start. You are to speak only when you're spoken to. And you're never, ever to question Mr. Bauer or me. Do you understand?"

"Yes," David said.

"That's 'yes, ma'am,' and 'yes, sir,' from now on," she snapped.

David quickly replied, "Yes, ma'am."

"Just don't forget," Mrs. Bauer said. She turned and spoke in low tones to Mr. Bauer.

A lump rose in David's throat as he thought about Mickey and his promise. So far David had seen no sign of kindness or humor or love in either Mr. or Mrs. Bauer.

Mickey wouldn't mislead me, he thought. *Maybe he just didn't know what parents were like.*

As the wagon bumped along, David began to notice the countryside. Stretches of dark forest gave way to open fields, still green under the summer sun. A stream bubbled through a pasture and under a wooden bridge, and a curious-looking animal with horns stuck its head over a fence to watch them.

"What is that?" David gasped.

"A cow," Mrs. Bauer said.

David pulled back, startled. He hadn't known cows were *that* big.

"David, we have a farmhand who has been with us for a little over a year," Mr. Bauer said, interrupting David's thoughts.

"Eighteen months," Mrs. Bauer said.

"Seventeen months, to be exact. His name is Amos Johnson, and he's an ex-slave," Mr. Bauer continued. He shook his head and grumbled, "Someone's hard-earned property."

Property? David didn't like the idea that a person should be thought of as someone else's property.

"Times are hard. Many men who ask for jobs are drifters. Maybe they stay a few weeks, maybe a few months. Then they move on. They get room and board and are paid in cash. You are not yet old enough or strong enough to take on some of the jobs these farmhands do. However, you can do enough of the chores to keep us from having to hire an extra man."

"Is that why you chose me?" David asked. "To be a farmhand? Will I be paid, too?"

Mrs. Bauer let out a squawk. "Of course not!" she said. "You lived on the streets of New York City, where you had nothing at all! We're giving you your own room—in the house, not the barn—a comfortable bed, and three good meals a day. And you ask for money! I can't believe it! What a greedy, greedy boy you are!"

Before David could answer, Mr. Bauer said, "These are the chores you will do each day. Do not forget them. You will be awakened at five. You will milk the cows twice a day, feed the hogs and cattle, feed and water the chickens, bring in the corncobs to burn in the cookstove, fill the wood box for the cooking and heating stoves, and fill the reservoirs on the stoves with water. You will wash and dry the dishes after each meal, put up the hay and alfalfa, clean the barn, and do whatever else you're called upon to do. Can you remember all that?"

David's head hurt. "I—I don't know, sir. I'll try. I'll do my best."

"Never mind," Mrs. Bauer said. She turned in her seat to fix David with another glare. "If you forget during the first few days, I'll remind you."

The lump came back into David's throat. "Some of the things you asked me to do . . . I don't know how to do them. I don't know how to milk a cow or how to feed chickens and cattle and hogs. I don't . . ." He stopped and thought a moment. "What *is* a hog?"

Mrs. Bauer sighed and said to her husband, "I told you so."

"I still think taking in an orphan boy was a good idea," Mr. Bauer said calmly. "You know I am usually right." He turned to look at David. "I told you I am a fair man. I will have Amos teach you all you need to know."

"Thank you . . . sir," David said.

"Hummph!" Mrs. Bauer grunted.

Mr. Bauer pulled the horses' reins to the right, and the wagon rumbled and bumped onto a narrow lane.

"There's the house," Mr. Bauer said as the wagon came to a stop.

David saw a large two-story house ahead of them. It was spotless white. A wide porch stretched across the front. David's eyes opened wide in surprise. It was a house for rich folk. It was even bigger and more beautiful than the brownstone homes in which the New York swells lived. This was going to be his new home? If Mickey could only see it!

For just an instant David felt a spark of hope. Mickey had said David's life would be better. And he'd said everything would turn out all right.

"Don't sit there daydreaming, David," Mrs. Bauer complained. "Hop out. And take your things with you. I'll show you your room. Then you can help me get supper ready."

"No, Sophie," Mr. Bauer said. "I'm going to take David around the farm and introduce him to Amos."

"You can do that later. I need his help now."

David felt a pain in his stomach. Were the Bauers always going to be like this? He squeezed his eyes shut. He wished he hadn't come west. He wished when he opened his eyes he'd be far away from here.

A soft, deep voice said, "Is this the boy?"

David's eyes flew open and he looked up into a smiling, kindly face.

"This is David Howard, Amos," Mr. Bauer said. "David, this is Amos Johnson, whom I told you about."

"Pleased to meet you, David," Amos said. He held out a large hand.

"I'm pleased to meet you, too, Mr. Johnson," David said, shaking Amos's hand.

Amos's smile grew wider. "Call me Amos, not

Mr. Johnson, and I'll call you David, not Mr. Howard. That's the way it is with friends."

"I'm glad we'll be friends," David said. "I had to leave my other friend. His name is Mickey."

"For goodness' sakes, stop wasting time!" Mrs. Bauer snapped. "There's things to do. Come with me, David! Right this minute!"

Chapter Five

David was shown to a small bedroom at the back of the house on the first floor. He ran his hands over the smooth blanket on the bed and gently touched the plump pillow. A real bed! A pillow all his own! He raised the pillow to his cheek.

"David! What are you doing? Get a move on!" Mrs. Bauer stood in the bedroom doorway, her voice as sharp as a needle. "I need your help in the kitchen."

David jumped and dropped the pillow. "Yes, ma'am," he said.

"Wash your hands and face first," Mrs. Bauer

told him. "I keep a clean kitchen, and I expect my help to be clean, too."

She was almost gone when she stopped and turned. "Oh, and put those shoes in the bottom drawer of the chest. You can save them for Sundays. They'll take longer to wear out that way. I don't intend to waste good money buying shoes."

David didn't mind. He was used to going barefoot.

He soon found that he liked working in the kitchen. As long as he did exactly what Mrs. Bauer told him to do, she kept her temper. Together they turned out a meal of roast beef, fried potatoes, turnips boiled with their greens, stewed tomatoes, and thick slices of white bread.

David's stomach rumbled in anticipation. "Mrs. Bauer, you must be the best cook in the whole world!" he blurted out.

Mrs. Bauer stopped, her arms filled with plates, and looked at David. For just an instant her face softened. "Twice in a row, in the years before the war, I entered my sponge cake at the county fair," she said. "Both times it won first place."

"I've seen sponges sold in stores," David said. "Wouldn't they be hard to eat?"

For just a moment Mrs. Bauer's lips twitched in a smile. "Get along with you," she said good-naturedly as she handed the plates to David. "Put these at Mr. Bauer's place at the end of the table. Then go find Amos and tell him to call the hands to supper."

"Yes, ma'am," David said. Excited about the wonderful meal he would soon be eating, he hurried to do just what Mrs. Bauer had said.

Amos and two other farmhands arrived at the back door, noisily splashing as they washed their faces, necks, and hands in the basin on the bench outside. The tall man was called John. The short man was called Clete. Both of them were sun-browned, muscular, and lean.

As soon as everyone had been seated, Mr. Bauer folded his hands, closed his eyes, and loudly said grace. David's stomach suddenly rumbled just as loudly. After a sharp look from Mrs. Bauer, David tried not to look at the food. He tried not to squirm in his chair. He tried to keep his mind on

Mr. Bauer's prayer. But the smell of all that good food was almost too tempting to resist.

When Mr. Bauer finally finished the prayer with a loud "Amen," David let out a long sigh of relief. He couldn't help it.

Mrs. Bauer flicked her napkin into her lap with a scowl. "You had better begin learning how to behave, David. It's easy to see that you didn't learn manners on those New York City streets."

Mr. Bauer frowned as he tucked one corner of his napkin into his collar. "Maybe as a lesson to you, David, you should leave the table," he said.

And miss eating all that good food? Terrified, David gripped the edge of the table. "I—I'm sorry, sir," he said.

Amos bent to look into David's eyes. "When's the last time you had somethin' to eat, David?" he asked.

"This morning, Mr. Johnson . . . Amos," David answered.

Amos smiled. "David's just hungry, Mr. Bauer. He had a long trip here and he's tired. You're known for bein' a fair man. You understand how a boy can feel."

Mr. Bauer nodded. He picked up the bowl of potatoes and spooned some onto one of the plates. "I *am* a fair man," he said. "So I'll overlook your behavior this time, David. Just don't let it happen again."

David was the last one served, and he smiled with delight at the heaping plate of food. His guess had been right. He'd eat well with the Bauers—as long as he was on his best behavior.

When David had almost finished, Mrs. Bauer said sternly, "Just so you'll know from the start, don't ask for seconds. I cook just enough to feed all of us comfortably, and I don't waste money. You won't find leftovers at *my* table. Also, don't be asking to eat between meals. Three good meals a day are all you or anybody else needs."

"Yes, ma'am," David said. He wondered if he was being scolded. Then he caught Amos's quick smile and wink and felt better. Mrs. Bauer probably said that all the time.

After dinner David washed the dishes. Mrs. Bauer bent over to check on him. "Do those plates again," she said. "Land sakes, boy, can't you see there's still crumbs stuck to a couple of them?"

"I'm sorry, ma'am. I didn't see them," David said. He held the plates near his face and peered at them, embarrassed when he saw the crumbs.

When he had finished he struggled to carry the big pan of soapy water outside. Mrs. Bauer showed him where to dump it—on the herb garden near the kitchen door.

"Soapsuds keep down the bugs," Mrs. Bauer explained.

David managed to fill the wood box and fill the reservoirs on the stoves with water. But it was hard to keep his eyes open. His head jerked as he fought sleep. He longed for his bed.

The sun still hadn't set when Mr. Bauer said, "We retire early, and we rise early. It is time for you to visit the privy, then go to bed."

He waited until David returned, then said, "Good night," and clumped up the stairs.

David made his way to his bedroom and sat on

the bed. The mattress was packed firmly with straw, and the sheets smelled of sunshine and fresh air. A real bed! And it was *his*!

Still dressed in the clothes he had worn on the train, David flopped onto the bed, exhausted. By the time his head touched the pillow he was sound asleep.

Chapter Six

"Wake up, David. Wake up!"

David struggled out of sleep, squirming away from the heavy hand that gripped his shoulder. For a moment he was back in New York City, and a policeman was chasing him away from the warm grate. He'd have to move fast or he'd feel the whack of the nightstick on his legs.

"David, you slept in your clothes. You will not do this again," a deep voice scolded. "You have a proper nightshirt for sleeping. It is in the chest of drawers."

A strong hand pulled David to his feet, and he opened his eyes. In the flickering lamplight he saw Mr. Bauer standing over him. David remembered coming to the Bauers' house, the meal, the chores. The chores! He'd have many more to do today. "I was so tired, sir. I meant to change out of my clothes, but—"

"It will not happen again."

"No, sir. I'm sorry, sir."

"Be ready for breakfast in ten minutes," Mr. Bauer said. He placed a flickering oil lamp on the high chest of drawers and strode from the room.

David didn't want to get into trouble again. He rushed to get ready and ran to the kitchen.

"Good morning," he said to Mrs. Bauer.

She nodded gruffly and gave him a searching look. " 'Good morning, *ma'am.*' Did you remember to wash?"

"Yes, ma'am," David said. The water in his pitcher and basin had been cold, but he liked the feeling of being clean. For almost as long as he could remember he had never thought about washing. Maybe if he'd had a mother he would have washed. But where he had lived, there were no mothers.

And there were no clothes to change into, either.

When his clothes grew too small or fell into rags, Mickey had managed to find him something else to wear. Even the shirts and trousers—and once, even a warm jacket—weren't new. And they weren't always clean when he got them. David had never asked where the clothes came from, and Mickey had never told him. David had to smile as he wondered what Mrs. Bauer would say about that.

Mrs. Bauer handed David a platter of fried eggs, their golden centers soft under a milky glaze. "Put this on the table," she ordered.

David's mouth watered. "Those are the most beautiful eggs I've ever seen."

"Hmmph. Flattery will get you nowhere," Mrs. Bauer grumped. But for just an instant she looked pleased.

David went back to the table with another platter, piled with crisp bacon and fat sausages, still sizzling from the pan. The next platter was heaped with golden-crusted biscuits. Mrs. Bauer added a large jar of peach preserves, a crock of butter, and a pitcher of milk to the table.

David was sure that none of the New York swells could eat any better than this. He greeted Amos, John, and Clete as they arrived, and sat very still during Mr. Bauer's morning prayer. David's mouth watered. But this time he didn't make a sound.

No one spoke during the meal, except to ask for the biscuits to be passed. The men ate quickly, taking huge bites.

David thought back to the train that had brought him west. The engine had a gaping hole, just like a mouth. Inside that mouth was a roaring fire. The fireman on the train had told David and some of the other boys that he had to shovel coal as fast as he could into that mouth to keep the fire going. "Engines need lots of fuel to keep them running," he'd explained.

I guess farmers need lots of fuel to keep working, David thought. He almost laughed aloud, thinking of Mr. Bauer, Amos, John, and Clete as big, shiny engines, huffing and puffing through the farm.

David suddenly noticed that the men had almost cleaned their plates. He was quick to shovel everything on his own plate into his mouth. He didn't want the Bauers to get angry with him again.

After breakfast David was sent with Amos to learn how to milk the cows.

"I'll show you how it's done," Amos said.

David hung back. "Cows are big," he whispered.

"They won't hurt you," Amos said. "C'mon. Watch what I do."

He hunkered down on the low wooden stool. "Rest your head against the cow's flank, like I'm doin'," he said, "and get a firm grip with both hands on two of her teats. Her udder is full of milk, so watch what I do." Twin streams of milk shot into the pail underneath.

"I want to try!" David said.

Amos moved from the stool and showed David how to place his fingers around the teats.

Impatiently David pulled on the teats, but no milk came out. Instead the cow bellowed, stepped sideways, and knocked David from his stool. His foot hit the bucket, and the milk spilled out.

David scrambled up, his heart thumping. "I

spilled the milk!" he cried. "Mr. Bauer will be angry!"

Amos patted David's shoulder. "Don't fret. Everybody makes mistakes when they're learnin'. Besides, there was only a little milk in that bucket."

Amos sat on the stool again. "Now, watch what I do with my fingers," he said. "Start squeezin' with the top finger and hold it as you move on down with the other fingers."

David knelt to watch. Amos's fingers were a blur, so David leaned forward, straining to see.

"Why're you squintin' like that?" Amos asked.

David sat back, surprised. "I was watching, like you said."

Amos chuckled. "You don't have to watch so hard. Just pay a mind to what I'm doin'."

David watched. Then he tried again. It wasn't as hard the second time. When he was able to send milk into the bucket, Amos laughed and said, "Good job, David." He clapped David on the back.

David felt as happy as when he'd done something to please Mickey.

Amos was patient and kind, and David worked hard to learn how to pour some of the milk into the separator, where the thick yellow cream could rise to the top. Each day he would skim off the cream, then pour it into a slender wooden churn. After the top was put on the churn, David clasped the pole that came out of a hole in the center of the top. Amos explained that at the bottom end of the pole were paddles. When the pole was pumped up and down, the paddles swished back and forth through the cream. This made the cream separate and grow thick with clumps of butter.

His arms aching from the churning, David scooped the butter into a bowl. Then he poured the leavings into a bucket.

Even if he was hungry, David would turn up his nose at the sour-smelling milk that had tiny specks of yellow butter floating in it.

Amos laughed. "That bad face you're makin'—that's exactly the same way I feel about buttermilk. I just never took to the taste."

David grinned. He liked sharing with Amos—

even if it was only their dislike for sour old buttermilk.

Feeding the chickens and gathering the eggs was easy, but David struggled with the heavy buckets filled with slop for the hogs to eat. He wrinkled his nose and tried not to breathe as he dumped the smelly slop into a long trough.

On Saturday evening David was handed a bitter-smelling lump of lye soap and was given a turn at a hot tub of water. The bath was a wonderful way to end the week. The next day he would go to church with the Bauers.

David had never been inside a church before. He liked the music and the singing, but he found he couldn't keep his mind on what the minister was saying. He hoped that the Bauers wouldn't notice that he hadn't paid attention.

After services, as David followed the Bauers outside, a boy his size stepped up to him. "Hello. I'm Fred Walker," the boy said. "You're the new orphan. I'm an orphan, too."

David looked at Fred with interest. "Did you come on an orphan train?"

"No," Fred said. "I live with my aunt and uncle, and I've been with them since I was a baby."

"I had a real mother and father when I was a baby," David said. He wished he could remember them. No matter how hard he tried, he couldn't picture their faces.

"I know a good fishing hole," Fred said. "Maybe you and me could go there someday. Or we could play marbles or mumbledypeg."

Before David could answer Mrs. Bauer interrupted. "David has too much work to do to waste time with play." She took David's hand and pulled him along as she greeted the other churchgoers. Most of them seemed nice. Some even introduced themselves to David.

But there were two men David didn't like—Barry Shiner and Augie Bean. Augie was tall and fair, with blotchy red skin. He had a way of sneaking looks from the corners of his eyes, and he paid no attention to David.

Barry was short and loud. Everyone could hear him as he said to Mr. Bauer, "You took in an orphan and got free farm labor. Smart move on your part."

Mrs. Bauer's face had turned red when Barry said that. After the Bauers had started their drive home, she said to Mr. Bauer, "There's something sneaky about Barry and Augie. I don't trust them."

"Don't be so quick to find fault. They come from good, solid, hardworking families," Mr. Bauer answered.

Mrs. Bauer sniffed. "Barry's been trouble since the day he was born. And Augie like to drove his schoolteacher to quit. It was a blessing to all of us when he dropped out of school and went off to join the Confederate Army."

"He fought bravely for the South. So did Barry. We owe them our gratitude for that. We can't hold a few youthful pranks against them."

"Youthful pranks?" Mrs. Bauer grumbled. "Say what you like in their favor. It don't change a thing. Nora Beemer was just telling me she's heard that this Ku Klux Klan thing is getting started in Harwood."

In Harwood? David thought with alarm.

"Nora says membership is supposed to be secret, but I'm sure those boys are members," Mrs. Bauer said. "Far as I can see, it's just one more way for the two of them to cause trouble."

"You shouldn't talk against the Klan. The way I understand it, they're simply trying to keep the South the way it used to be," Mr. Bauer said. "The Southern states were badly hurt during the war. President Johnson has taken away property and . . ."

Mr. Bauer went on to talk about the problems faced by the Southern states, but David stopped listening. He didn't want to hear about the Klan. The people in it hated other people only because they had dark skin. They hated people like Mickey, who was a good friend to everybody. Maybe there were people in New York City who worried about what color skin other people had, but David and Mickey hadn't cared or even thought about it. And no one ever tried to stop them from being friends.

The people in the Klan hate people like Amos too,

David realized. He decided that the people who joined the Klan must be both mean and stupid. And it frightened David to think that the Klan could be so close to where he lived . . . and Amos.

Chapter Seven

For the first few evenings it was hard for David to stay awake long enough to wash his hands, face, and neck and put on his nightshirt.

But as time went on he found that he woke early, often before he heard Mr. Bauer's heavy footsteps coming down the stairs. And when it was time for bed he sometimes wasn't even sleepy.

David enjoyed the farm chores. He even got used to feeding the hogs. Clete and John praised him. Amos told him he was the best worker he'd ever known. Their compliments made David feel good about himself, but he wished there were some way he could satisfy Mr. and Mrs. Bauer.

"Look at you, David," Amos said. "Liftin' those

heavy buckets almost like they was empty. Three weeks ago you couldn't have done that."

David tried to smile. "Mr. Bauer said I wasn't getting my chores done fast enough. I can't seem to please him . . . or Mrs. Bauer, either."

"So that's why you got a long face," Amos said. He chuckled. "Don't worry about pleasin' the Bauers. Nobody pleases 'em. They seem to like it that way."

David picked up the two empty buckets. But before he carried them to the pump to be washed he said, "It isn't just the Bauers. Sometimes I work so hard I forget about Mickey, but when I do think about him I miss him so much my stomach hurts."

"It's like that with friends," Amos said.

"Mickey told me I'd make new friends," David said, "but I don't know how. Mrs. Bauer told me I had too much work to do. I couldn't waste time with play."

"You'll make new friends," Amos promised. "And you'll never forget your old ones."

David thought about that for a moment before

he told Amos: "Mickey always told me, 'Look up. Look up at the stars and you'll be all right.' "

"That sounds like mighty good advice," Amos said. "Your friend Mickey knew what he was talkin' about."

David was surprised. "Do you look up at the stars too?"

"Sometimes that's the only place *to* look," Amos answered. "Those stars make all the miseries down here on earth seem a lot smaller. Ain't that right?"

David was afraid to tell Amos that he didn't really understand. All David could see was a blur in the sky. What was so good about that? *Is there something wrong with me?* David wondered. *Why can't I see what Mickey and Amos see?*

For a few moments Amos was silent. Then he said, "Do you like storytellin'?"

"Storytelling? What's that?"

Amos smiled. "It's when all of us hired hands sit around in the barn together before we turn in for the night. We swap stories about what we've seen, where we've been, and where we're goin'. Why don't you join us?"

"I will!" David's heart jumped with excitement.

Amos put a hand on David's arm. "Just don't be tellin' the Bauers," he said softly. "Understand?"

"I understand."

"Tonight," Amos said.

"Tonight," David whispered.

David heard the kitchen door open and Mrs. Bauer shout, "David? Where are you?"

"Here I am!" David called. "I'll be there soon as I wash the buckets." He ran, the buckets banging against his legs. He was eager for nighttime and the storytelling to come.

That evening, as soon as Mr. Bauer had climbed the stairs, David opened his window wide. Even though it was not yet dark, he wasn't worried that he'd be seen by Mr. or Mrs. Bauer. The Bauers' bedroom was at the front of the house. And once they had settled down for the night they didn't stir. But he did have to be careful that they didn't hear the loud squeak of the window sash as it was shoved up or down.

David climbed over the windowsill and jumped to the ground below. He'd have to leave his window open. That meant a few mosquitoes, June bugs, and moths might decide to fly in. He shrugged. He'd worry about that when he returned.

As quietly as possible, he ran to the barn and slipped through the partly open door. In the tack room a lantern gleamed. David headed toward its light. He greeted Amos, Clete, and John, who were seated on the hard-packed dirt floor.

"Sit down, David," Amos said. He patted the floor, and David joined him.

John paused to say hello to David. Then he went on with what he'd been saying. "I gotta admit that Mrs. Bauer is a mighty good cook. I'm gonna miss her cookin' when I move on."

Startled, David asked, "Why are you moving on? If you like Mrs. Bauer's cooking, why don't you just stay here?"

John shook his head. "There's a lot of world out there. If I stay in any one place too long, I'll miss seein' the rest of it."

Clete chuckled and said to David, "John's a drifter. So am I. Drifters gotta keep movin' on."

"All we want is a few weeks' pay and food to fill our bellies," John explained.

"All across the county there's nothin' much else besides farmwork in the way of jobs. Lots of folk can't find work of any kind," Clete said.

"We don't own much. And we don't need much. What we got we keep in our knapsacks. That makes it easy to pick up and move whenever we get the urge," John said. "As for me, I'll soon be headin' for California." He looked at Amos. "Seems to me you'd be better off out in California, too."

"What's California got that I ain't got right here where I am?" Amos asked.

"It's what California *hasn't* got, and that's the Klan," John answered.

"I'm not afraid of the Klan," Amos said. "I keep to myself and don't bother nobody. So nobody's gonna bother me."

"Don't be so sure," Clete told him. "I heard the Klan's already reached Harwood."

David glanced at Amos. He didn't want Amos to get hurt by the Klan. But he didn't want Amos to go to California either. He'd already lost his friend Mickey. He didn't want to lose Amos, too.

All the time Clete was talking about the Klan, Amos didn't lose his easy smile. "I'm not worried. Harwood folk don't have nothin' against me," Amos said.

"They might, if they get themselves riled up," John said. "If I was you I'd get clear of 'em. Go out to California, like me. I'm gonna look for gold, get rich, and buy me a diamond stickpin."

John smiled and continued. "I heard about a man who joined the rush to California in forty-nine, lookin' for gold. He found a nugget at the edge of a stream. That nugget was so big that when he tried to pull it out of the ground it came loose and fell on him. It took three men and a mule to pull that nugget offa him. That nugget was too heavy to haul off in a wagon, so that man come up with the idea of rollin' that gold nugget all the way to the bank in the nearest town."

"Did he get it there?" David asked.

"Yes, he did," John said. "But rollin' it up and down those mountains till he got to town didn't do the nugget no good. By the time he got to the bank, that big old gold nugget had wore itself down till it was no bigger'n a marble."

Everyone laughed, and Clete said, "He was just lucky the bears didn't get him. There's bears bigger'n horses in California. They're mean and fierce too. A man I know got chased by a bear in California and tried to save hisself by climbin' a tree. But that old bear come right up the tree after him. The man climbed higher 'n' higher, but so did the bear. Luckily, at the top of the tree was an eagle's nest. The man grabbed the eagle's legs, and that eagle took off and flew the man away from the bear to another tree. I talked to the man myself so I know the story's true."

David listened to Clete's story with delight. What an exciting and dangerous place California must be! He wished he could dig for gold nuggets and fight fierce bears and fly with eagles. "Don't stop. Tell more stories," David begged when Clete stood up and stretched.

But Amos shook his head. "You know we gotta rise early," he said. "Time now to get some sleep."

"Can I come back tomorrow night?" David asked.

"We'll be expectin' you," Amos said.

It was dark by the time David climbed back into his bedroom. He quickly pulled on his nightshirt and climbed into bed. After swatting two mosquitoes that whined past his ears, he settled down to sleep.

But he couldn't. Instead, he stared into the darkness, wide awake. What the men had said about the Ku Klux Klan being in Harwood worried him. He didn't want the Klan to hurt Amos. *But they'd have no reason to harm a man so good and kind,* he reasoned. *Would they?*

Chapter Eight

Two days later John left the Bauers' farm. That afternoon Mr. Bauer drove into town and returned with a young man whose skin was even darker than Amos's. He carried his belongings in a feed sack that was slung over his shoulder. He spoke so softly that David couldn't hear him, and he kept his eyes on the ground.

Mr. Bauer called to Amos. When Amos came from the barn the young man looked up for the first time. When he saw Amos, he suddenly looked hopeful.

"Amos, this is Isaac," Mr. Bauer said. "Amos, show Isaac around the farm. Tell him what he'll need to do."

Mr. Bauer turned to David. "Why aren't you busy, David?" he asked.

David jumped. "I just brought a load of corncobs to the stove," he answered. "I stopped to meet Isaac."

Mr. Bauer grunted, "You've met him. So now get busy . . . all of you."

Once they were inside the barn, David told Isaac his name.

"You the master's son?" Isaac asked David.

Amos quickly spoke up. "Mr. Bauer's not your master. And you ain't a slave anymore. The United States government made us free citizens."

"And I'm not Mr. Bauer's son," David said. "I'm an orphan. The Bauers took me in."

For the first time Isaac smiled at David. "You and me got somethin' in common. I know what it's like not to have parents."

"You're an orphan, too?"

Isaac shrugged. "I don't know. Might never know. I figure I was around eight years old or so when I was taken from my mama and sold."

David suddenly felt sick to his stomach. Sold!

What a horrible way to lose a mother and father! "Can't you try to find your parents?" he asked.

"I tried," Isaac said. "That old plantation where they lived got burned to the ground during the fightin'. Nobody who had worked there was left. And nobody in town could tell me anythin' about where my mama and papa coulda gone." He sadly shook his head. "I got no family. I got no home."

"You got a home now," Amos said. "Long as you get your work done, Mr. Bauer will keep you on." Amos turned to David. "That means you, too, David."

David hurried to fill his sack again with dried corncobs from the bin against the far wall. He hoisted the heavy sack and struggled toward the kitchen.

He was surprised to hear voices in the parlor, which Mrs. Bauer kept dusted and polished and ready for visitors. David was curious, so he peeked through the open doorway to see who the visitors were.

When he saw that Barry Shiner and Augie Bean

were seated on the dark red, plush sofa, David quickly backed into the kitchen, out of sight.

The clock in the hall struck the quarter hour. David heard Mrs. Bauer say, "It's nigh on noon, and we'll be sitting down to eat. Care to join us for dinner?"

Barry's voice was sharp as he answered, "No. We hear you don't care who sits at your table."

Mrs. Bauer gasped. "Wh-What?"

"Like some of your hired help."

Mr. Bauer bellowed, "Our farmhands eat with us in the kitchen, if that is what you mean."

David heard the anger in Mrs. Bauer's voice when she snapped, "Barry Shiner, your ma serves farmhands in the kitchen, too. I know this for a fact, so don't tell me different."

"Our help is people like us," Barry said.

"Which is why we're payin' you this call," Augie broke in. "We heard you done give another job to a Negro. That makes two of 'em you're payin' wages to."

"Two jobs which coulda gone to white folk," Barry added. "That's not good, Mr. Bauer."

David shivered as Mr. Bauer's voice grew even louder. "I hire men who will be able to give me a full day's work," he said. "I want honest value for my money. That's all that matters."

"Maybe you better think more about *who* you hire," Augie said.

"And maybe you boys just better think about behaving yourselves," Mrs. Bauer said shrilly. "I'm going to have a talk with your mother, Augie Bean. And yours too, Barry Shiner."

"The Klan don't like—" Augie began.

"Don't tell us what the Klan likes or doesn't like," Mr. Bauer interrupted. "Are you telling me that the Klan has no regard for personal privacy? What we do is none of anyone else's business—the Klan's or yours."

"We're just sayin' that—"

"Leave," Mr. Bauer rumbled. "We have nothing more to talk about."

David slipped out the back door of the house and ran to the woodpile to split kindling. The Bauers were plenty angry with Barry and Augie, and rightly so. David knew better than to be around either of the Bauers until they'd had time to cool off. He didn't want them to be mad at him, too.

From listening to Clete and John, David knew that times were hard and many men didn't have jobs. But he also knew that Barry and Augie didn't visit the Bauers because they were worried about local people finding work. Mickey had told him that the members of the Klan hated people with dark skin. Barry and Augie seemed to be filled with this hatred too.

Wiping the sweat from his forehead, David stopped to rest and think. Mr. and Mrs. Bauer may have stopped Augie and Barry for now, but David was afraid that the two men weren't through causing trouble. What they'd said had been a warning to the Bauers.

What was going to happen to Amos? And now Isaac, too?

Chapter Nine

Clete came into the barn with the weekly *Harwood Journal* the next day and handed it to Amos. "There's a story on the front page of this newspaper," he said. "It's about the Klan here in Harwood. Maybe John was right, Amos. Maybe you ought to pack up and head for California. Isaac, too."

Before Amos could answer, Clete left to tend to the horses. Amos studied the newspaper. "Guess I should know what that news story says," he told David. "But I can't read. Can you?"

"Yes," David answered.

"Then will you read me what it says about the Ku Klux Klan?"

David took the paper. He held it closer and closer, until the letters stopped blurring together. He slowly read aloud. " 'The secret society known as the Ku Klux Klan has formed a chapter here in Harwood. Organized in the South by ex-Confederates and led by Nathan B. Forrest, it has spread—' "

"Stop," Amos interrupted. "Why're you holdin' that paper practically up against your nose?"

"So I can see the words," David said.

Amos moved the newspaper back. "Can you see them now?"

David squinted, but the letters still ran together. "No," he said.

Amos pointed at a sack of feed on a nearby shelf. "Read me what's written on the side of that sack over there."

With his eyes almost shut from squinting, David strained to see. "I can't," he said.

"There's a pitchfork hanging on a hook over on the far wall," Amos said. "How many tines has it got?"

David saw only blurry shapes. He couldn't tell which was the pitchfork and which were other tools. "Four?" he guessed.

"That one's got only three," Amos said. He shook his head. "David, boy, you don't see the way you should."

"I see just like everybody else does . . . don't I?"

"No, you don't. But somethin' can be done about it. You need a pair of spectacles."

"What are spectacles?"

"Eyeglasses. You've seen people wearing eyeglasses, haven't you?"

"Old people. Not any children." Not really sure that Amos was right, David said, "Besides, I haven't got any money. So where am I going to get spectacles?"

"We'll tell the Bauers you need 'em. They took you to raise, so it's up to them to take care of your needs. And it looks to me like you're in real need of spectacles."

———

Just before Mr. and Mrs. Bauer prepared to lock up the house and send David off to bed, Amos knocked at the kitchen door.

"I'd like to speak with you, Mrs. Bauer," Amos said, as she opened the door. "And with your husband, too, ma'am, if that's agreeable to you both."

Mrs. Bauer sighed. "Land sake, Amos. Come in. What's so important that it can't wait till morning?"

Mr. Bauer joined them quickly in the kitchen. David followed.

"Amos, you're not going to tell me that you're leaving, are you?" Mr. Bauer began. "I count on you. You're the best farmhand I've ever had. If you're worried about those stupid boys with their foolish talk about the Ku Klux Klan—"

"No, sir," Amos said. "That's not what I want to talk about. I'm well satisfied here."

"Well, then?" Mrs. Bauer snapped. "We can't stand here chatting all night."

Amos cleared his throat. "It's about David."

"David?" Mr. Bauer stared down at David, and

David backed up until he felt the support of the wall behind him. "What's David done wrong?"

"He hasn't done nothin' wrong," Amos said. "David's a fine worker and a good boy."

"Then what—?"

"I asked David to read somethin' to me," Amos said. "He had to hold that paper right up to his nose to see it. I tested him on readin' a few other things, and it's clear that boy has poor eyesight. He needs spectacles."

"Spectacles?" Mrs. Bauer screeched.

"For a boy David's age? That's ridiculous," Mr. Bauer said. "Spectacles are for the elderly."

"They're for people who can't see, no matter their age," Amos said.

"You're no doctor, Amos," Mrs. Bauer insisted. "You can't even read. How could you know enough to say that boy needs spectacles?"

"Ask him to read somethin', please, Mrs. Bauer," Amos said. "You'll see how David has to hold the paper close, else he can't see it."

Mr. Bauer scowled. "Just where's the money supposed to come from to pay for spectacles?"

"Spectacles don't cost much," Amos said. "A man I know told me they got a box of 'em down at the dry goods store. He got a fine lookin' pair of gold-rimmed eyeglasses just by tryin' 'em on until he found one that was right for his eyes."

"Nonsense!" Mr. Bauer said. "We don't need you to put notions in the boy's head. What would he need spectacles for around here anyway? Will the spectacles help him get more milk from the cows? Or carry a sack of corncobs without dropping it?"

"They certainly won't," Mrs. Bauer snapped. "Matter of fact, being a boy, he'd probably break the spectacles the first week he had them. He's doing fine without them."

Mr. Bauer said firmly, "Waste greenbacks on a needless pair of spectacles? Maybe you have the money, Amos, but we haven't. I don't want to hear any more about spectacles, do you understand?"

"Yes, sir," Amos said. He sent a sorrowful look to David, then turned and left the kitchen.

"Imagine that!" Mrs. Bauer exclaimed. "Imagine

a hired hand having the nerve to tell us what we should or shouldn't do!"

Mr. Bauer leaned down to stare at David, whose heart thumped loudly. "There will be no more talk about spectacles, David," Mr. Bauer said. "Is that understood?"

"Yes, sir," David whispered. One Bauer mad at him was bad enough. With both of them angry, he didn't dare say a word more.

Chapter Ten

The next morning Amos arrived at the woodpile while David was busy splitting logs. He took the ax from David and finished the job with a few strong blows.

"You got some time to spare now, so come with me," Amos said. "I gotta take the horses to the blacksmith in Harwood to get 'em shod. I told Mr. Bauer I needed your help, so he said you could come along."

Eagerly David helped hitch the horses to the wagon.

As he began to climb into the back, Amos said, "Up here, David. You ride on the seat alongside me."

Perched high on the board seat, David took a deep breath. The air smelled of horses' sweat and grasses warmed by the sun.

Amos told David about when he was a boy, working as a slave on a plantation in Georgia. And David told Amos about when he lived in New York City and slept on the streets.

"One good thing about bein' at the bottom—the only place to go is up," Amos said, chuckling.

David smiled. "You sound like Mickey. He said everything that happens has a good side."

"I think I'd like your friend Mickey," Amos said.

"Mickey would like you, too," David replied, imagining his two good friends together.

Before long they were close to Harwood. Amos pulled some folded bills from the pocket of his jacket and handed them to David. "Take these greenbacks," he said. "Afore I leave off the horses, we're gonna see about gettin' you those spectacles."

David stiffened. "We can't. Mr. Bauer said he didn't want to hear any more talk about spectacles.

If I come home with some, what's he going to say?"

"What Mr. and Mrs. Bauer's got to say has already been said. Don't you remember Mr. Bauer tellin' me that maybe I got the money to buy spectacles, but he don't? To my way of thinkin' he give me the go-ahead."

"I don't want you to get into trouble, Amos," David said. "I see just fine the way I am."

"I thank you for thinkin' of me," Amos said. "But you *don't* see just fine. You don't know what it's like to see the way you should."

They entered the main street of Harwood. Amos pulled the horses to a halt in front of the dry goods store. "Here we are," he said to David. "Hop out."

David was surprised. "You're coming with me, aren't you?" he asked.

"It's better I don't," Amos said. "Mr. Krane don't much like my kind of people in his store."

David shook his head. "Then I won't go in, either."

"Yes, you will, because I want you to," Amos answered. "You ask Mr. Krane to help you, and he'll do a good job findin' you the right pair of spectacles."

As David slid to the edge of the seat, ready to climb from the wagon, Amos added, "Just don't tell Mr. Krane where the money come from. It's better if he thinks Mr. Bauer give it to you."

David had been inside Mr. Krane's store with Mrs. Bauer before, when she had brought him along to carry her parcels. David quietly entered the store and made his way to where Mr. Krane stood behind a counter. A few wisps of gray hair stuck out over each of Mr. Krane's ears, and they trembled as he peered at David.

"Ah, it's the Bauers' orphan boy," he said. "What can I do for you?"

David took a deep breath. He clasped his hands together to keep them from shaking. He hoped Mr. Krane wouldn't ask where he'd got the money. He didn't want to get Amos in trouble, but he didn't want to lie. "I—I don't see as good as I should," he said. "I need a pair of spectacles."

Mr. Krane led David to the far end of one of the counters. Behind a box with rows of spectacles in it was a printed card. He picked it up and handed it to David. "Read this," he said.

David held the card up to his nose and read the first line.

"My, my, my," Mr. Krane said. "It's plain you *do* need spectacles." He fished through the rows of spectacles with their round, gold-framed lenses and pulled out a pair. "Try these," he said to David.

David put on the spectacles and looked up at Mr. Krane. Gasping, David jumped back. Mr. Krane's face stood out so clearly that David could see the wart on his forehead and the white hairs sprouting from his nose.

He slowly turned, staring at everything in the store. On the shelves pots and pans gleamed. Bolts of cloth shone in blues, yellows, and reds. And the glass in the big front window glittered under its light coating of dust. "Is this what seeing is like?" David whispered to himself.

"Makes a difference, doesn't it?" Mr. Krane answered, and David could hear the pleasure in his voice. "I guess I picked the right pair for you. Well, I'll just put this on the Bauers' bill."

"No!" David cried out, startling Mr. Krane. He quickly held out the bills Amos had given him. "I've got the money right here," he said. "Is this enough?"

Mr. Krane took the greenbacks and nodded. "Earned it yourself, did you? Well, you've got some change coming."

David slowly walked toward the door. His mouth fell open with surprise as he studied the details in a painting of a vase of flowers. Excitedly, he picked up a book with a red leather cover. The story wasn't very interesting, but the words stood out clearly. David was amazed. *Reading isn't hard when you can see the words,* he thought.

As he left the store he saw Amos waiting for him on the street. He ran to Amos, shouting, "Look, Amos! Look at my spectacles! I can see things I never saw before! I can see!"

Amos grinned and grabbed David's shoulders. "Those spectacles look mighty fine on you, too. You look like a regular schoolteacher or a doctor."

David studied his friend's face. For the first time he could see the laugh lines around Amos's mouth and the warmth in his eyes. "I didn't know what it would be like to see everything. I can read words better, too."

He was suddenly jostled from behind and shoved aside. He caught his balance and looked up to see Barry Shiner and Augie Bean.

"Ain't that old Amos?" Barry asked Augie. "Don't he belong down to the Bauer place?"

Amos stood silently, and Barry took another step toward him. "Whatcha doin' hangin' around here?" Barry asked Amos.

"Maybe he's thinkin' of stealin' somethin' from Krane's store," Augie said.

"Maybe he stole somethin' from the Bauers already," Barry said.

Two women stopped and turned to look at Amos.

David hurried to defend Amos. "That's not true," he insisted. "Amos didn't steal anything. He brought Mr. Bauer's horses to the blacksmith's."

"It's the orphan boy," Barry said to Augie, and laughed. "Take a look at him. He's wearin' spectacles. Where'd you get those, orphan boy? Did you sneak 'em out of Mr. Krane's store?"

"No! Amos bought them for me," David answered before he could stop himself.

Augie plucked the glasses from David's face. "Amos bought you these? How come he's spending greenbacks on eyeglasses for you? Probably stole the money in the first place."

David reached for his spectacles, but Augie held them even higher out of reach.

"Amos didn't steal the money! It's his own money!" David cried. "Amos bought me the spectacles because the Bauers wouldn't!"

Augie and Barry looked at each other. Then Barry took another step toward Amos. "What's the matter with you, old man? Tryin' to shame good white folks, are you?"

David was aware that a few more people had stopped to watch and listen. Amos's face was tight with fear. David was really scared now.

"Leave Amos alone!" he told Barry.

Augie giggled and waved the spectacles over

his head. "I think we got to teach old Amos a lesson—and you, too, orphan boy," he said. "You might like to see how easy these eyeglasses can break."

"No!" David burst into tears. "Please!"

Chapter Eleven

Like a gust of wind, the two women who had been watching charged into the group. One waved her closed umbrella like a club. She snatched the spectacles away from Augie and handed them to David. "You'll do no such thing, Augie Bean," she snapped. "You may not believe what this boy told you, but we do." She looked at her friend, and the two women nodded. "We know the Bauers."

Augie backed away, his eyes on the umbrella, but he kept arguing. "Where'd Amos get the money to buy those spectacles? He had to get it from someplace."

The woman said, "He works and gets paid for

his work. That's more than either of you've a mind to do. Now, get along—both of you! And if you give Amos or the Bauers or this fine boy any trouble, I'll have the sheriff on you!"

"We'll see about that," Barry muttered. "The Bauers have been askin' for trouble." But he and Augie quickly walked away.

The woman with the umbrella shook her head sadly. "Better stay away from those two trouble-makers," she said. "There's no telling what they'll take a notion to do."

David and Amos thanked the women and walked toward the blacksmith's shop.

David stopped as they came to a large redbrick building with wide steps and a large front door. He remembered what Miss Kelly had told him just before he left with the Bauers. "That's the court-house, isn't it?" he asked. "It's where I can find Judge Winters."

"What you want with a judge?" Amos asked.

"Miss Kelly told me if I needed help I could go to Judge Winters."

"I don't think that—" Amos began.

"I'll meet you at the blacksmith's shop," David called over his shoulder, as he ran up the steps to the courthouse.

Judge Winters wasn't in court. He sat in a small office with his feet propped on his desk. Even though Miss Kelly had pointed him out when they came to Harwood, for the first time David could see clearly what Judge Winters looked like. He was as sunburnt as any farmer, but he didn't wear farmers' clothes. He wore a black suit and a shirt with a high collar, like the swells in New York City. His boots were the shiniest black David had ever seen, with fancy stitching around the toes.

David told the Judge about Augie and Barry and what they had said about the Ku Klux Klan.

Judge Winters nodded and listened until David had finished. Then he dropped his feet to the floor and leaned toward David. "The Klan's mighty secret about who belongs to it. If I were you I wouldn't try to guess, and I wouldn't say what I was thinking. Understand?"

"But I don't want them to hurt Amos . . . or Isaac," David insisted.

"Don't worry, boy," Judge Winters said. "You just go home to the Bauers. I'll take care of things."

"Thank you," David said. He hoped the judge would keep his promise. There was nothing else he could do.

David and Amos were silent as they got the horses and hitched them to the wagon. As they drove out of town Amos glanced from side to side. Once in a while he twisted around to look behind them. It wasn't until they were well away from Harwood that Amos seemed to relax.

David said, "Barry and Augie belong to the Ku Klux Klan."

Amos looked at him with surprise. "They say so?"

"No, but I'm pretty sure," David said. "I was in the kitchen when they came to the house the other day. I couldn't help hearing what they talked about. They said that the Klan didn't like Mr. Bauer hiring Isaac . . . and you."

As Amos sighed and shook his head, David

asked, "Why do they hate so much? Why do people want to hate other people?"

"I don't know," Amos answered. "I guess that some people are so sour inside, hate's all they got left."

"Are you scared of them?"

"I was scared of what they might do, bein' riled up like they was," Amos said. "But I'm not scared now. Spendin' your life bein' scared does no good. And hatin' people in return makes you no better than them."

"I can't help being scared," David answered. "I don't want anything bad to happen to you."

For a while Amos was silent. Then he said, "Your friend Mickey had the right idea."

David was puzzled. "What idea?"

Amos smiled. "Think on it. It's somethin' you told me."

David shook his head. "I don't know what you mean."

"You'll know soon enough. Tonight, after everyone's in bed and it's good and dark, meet me outside. I'll show you what I mean."

"What are we going to do?"

"Wait and see," Amos said. "Be sure to bring your spectacles with you. Meet me by the barn."

David bounced on the wagon seat. "Then what?"

"Never you mind," Amos said. "Just be there."

David's heart beat faster. What did Amos have in mind? And why should it be secret?

A thought suddenly shocked David. Mickey had told him to go west. Maybe Amos was going to go west too—to California. And maybe he was going to take David with him!

Chapter Twelve

Afraid that his spectacles would cause trouble, David hid them from the Bauers. He raced through his chores and gulped down his supper, eager for bedtime to arrive.

As soon as it was dark, David climbed out his bedroom window. The moon was full, lighting the way. He put on his spectacles, and to his delight, he could see clearly as he raced to the barn.

Amos sat waiting for him in the tack room. "Where are Clete and Isaac?" David asked.

"Clete's bedded down, and Isaac . . . well, it was best for Isaac that he move on. That boy will find a better life when he gets out west."

David gasped. "He left because of the Klan, didn't he? Why didn't you go, too?"

"Because there's somethin' I gotta do first."

David grabbed Amos's arm. "When you leave I'll go with you. I don't own much. I can pack my things in a minute."

Amos shook his head. "Livin' on the road's no life for a boy," he said. "Besides, we're not runnin' and we're not hidin'. You and me are just goin' on a walk."

"A walk?" David was puzzled.

"Come with me," Amos said. He snuffed out the lantern. "You'll see what I mean."

From the back of the barn Amos led David down a path through a pasture and into a thin patch of woods. Two squirrels dashed across their path, and David could see the bright shine of their eyes. He held his breath as a rabbit, brown as the underbrush, sat up, alert.

The path became steep and led upward. When they reached a small clearing at the top of the hill, Amos said, "Here's where we stop. Look around you."

David sucked in his breath. The summer air was so clear in the moonlight that David felt he could almost touch the fragile, shivering tops of the trees that edged the hill across the way. A lake shimmered below. Silvery ripples of moonlight stretched across it like a ribbon.

"Look up, David," Amos whispered. "What do you see?"

David raised his eyes to the dark sky. It was dotted with millions of twinkling, gleaming lights.

"Amos!" David cried. "The stars! I can see the stars!"

For nearly an hour David and Amos lay on their backs, watching the night sky. David began to relax. Inside that vast sweep of beauty his problems with the Bauers seemed very small. The smaller the problems grew, the surer David became that he could handle those problems.

"Now I know why Mickey told me to look up at the stars," David said. He touched his spectacles and smiled. "This time I can really see them."

Amos and David headed for home, but as they came close to the farm they heard the sound of horses and voices. They sneaked into the darkened barn through the back door and ran to the front, where they peered through a slat in the door.

Men, wearing white robes and white, peaked hoods sat astride their horses, facing Mr. Bauer. Some of them held torches. Two of them carried coils of rope.

"The Klan!" Amos whispered.

David was so frightened, it was hard to breathe.

Mr. Bauer shouted, "Why don't you leave? You've searched the barn. You know that Amos and Isaac have gone." His voice was angry.

"Lucky for them they lit outta here," one of the riders called. David gasped when he realized it was Barry's voice. "There wasn't no call for Amos to be rude to upstandin', law-abidin' citizens, like he was in town today."

David clenched his fists. He whispered to Amos, "You weren't rude! *He* was! He's lying!"

"Hush," Amos said. He held a finger to his lips.

"Amos was the best farmhand I've ever had!" Mr. Bauer sputtered. "And you've driven him away!"

"Don't you care that he stole your money and shamed you by buyin' eyeglasses for your orphan boy?" yelled a voice that was clearly Augie's.

There was a moment of silence, during which David held his breath. Then Mr. Bauer shouted, "Amos did not steal my money! This is my business, not yours!"

David sighed in relief. He whispered to Amos, "I'll take one of the horses. I'll ride to town and get Judge Winters. He'll help us."

He was about to leave when he heard another familiar voice. It came from a nearby rider. "Maybe some of the boys got a little too excited about those spectacles, Elmer. But take this as a warning. Be careful who you hire."

In the light from the torches David could see the gleam on the boots of that rider. The boots were new and highly polished. There was fancy stitching around the toes. They looked exactly like the boots Judge Winters had been wearing. David was in despair. The rider had to be Judge Winters.

David tried not to cry as he told Amos, "There's nobody to help us."

"Then we help ourselves," Amos whispered. He bent close to David's ear. "I'll be goin'. I didn't want to, but I got no choice now."

"I want to go with you."

"No," Amos said firmly. "Right now your place is here. The Bauers ain't the kindest of people, but they've given you a home and they'll feed you well. Mr. Bauer tries to be a fair man. You heard him stand up for me to the Klan."

"You can't go, Amos!" David cried. "I can't stay here without you!"

"Of course you can," Amos answered. "You're a smart boy, and you've got plenty of gumption."

"What's gumption?" David asked.

"Spirit, David. Spirit and courage. Look how you faced up to Barry and Augie when we was in town."

"If you stay Mr. Bauer and I will keep standing up for you."

"It won't be enough." Amos squatted so that he could look into David's eyes. "You and I both know that runnin' away don't solve problems. But people like me can't defend themselves against riled up, noose-carryin' Klansmen. The only thing to do for now is to get out of their way. Do you understand?"

A hard lump rose in David's throat. He realized in sorrow that unlike Amos, he had a choice of leaving or staying. And, much as he wanted to be with Amos, David knew the right choice for him would be to stay. "I understand," he answered, "but I'm going to miss you."

"Then do what Mickey told you," Amos said. "Look at the stars. They're the same stars that'll shine down on Mickey in New York City and on me, wherever I might be. You think of me, and I'll think of you."

Before David could answer, Amos had slipped away through the darkness of the barn.

Wiping away his tears, David waited until the members of the Klan rode off. When all was silent, he left the barn.

Mrs. Bauer sat on the front porch steps and wept. Mr. Bauer slumped next to her. "What can we do? What can we do against those terrible men?" he kept repeating.

Chapter Thirteen

David stopped when he reached the foot of the steps. "Amos didn't want to go away, Mr. Bauer," David said. "He liked working here. But the Klan wouldn't let him stay."

Startled, the Bauers stared at David.

Finally Mrs. Bauer said, "So those are the spectacles that caused all the trouble!"

"The spectacles didn't cause trouble. It's the hating that caused it, and hating is going to keep causing trouble," David said. His knees shook a little as he faced Mr. Bauer, but he had to speak his piece. "You stood up for Amos. Just like he said, you *are* a fair man."

For a moment Mr. Bauer looked flustered.

"Amos said that? Well, he was right. I *did* stand up for him, didn't I?"

"Huh!" Mrs. Bauer sniffed. "You said what you did because you didn't want those Klansmen poking their noses into your business."

David didn't want the Bauers to argue again. Not now. He quickly said, "Amos was right about the spectacles, too. I can see a lot better. I can even see the stars."

"See the stars?" Mrs. Bauer sniffed. "What kind of foolishness is that?"

"It's what my friend Mickey told me to do when I had troubles," David said.

"The stars can't do anything about the troubles we have," Mr. Bauer complained.

"But looking at them can help you think about what to do," David said.

"There's nothing *anyone* can do against the Klan."

David took a deep breath. He had been surprised when Amos had told him he had gumption. Now he stood as tall as he could. He *did* have gumption. He didn't know where it had come from, but it was there. Maybe some had come from Amos and some from Mickey. Maybe some gumption had been there inside himself all the time.

"There *is* something that can be done," David declared. "If enough *good* people stick together, they won't have to put up with the Klan."

Mr. Bauer grunted. "Be practical, boy. I have a farm to take care of."

"There are other men who'll need jobs, and you can hire them," David said. "And I'm here to help you. I'm growing bigger and stronger, and I can learn to do more of the heavy farm chores."

"Yes," Mr. Bauer said. He stroked his chin as he studied David. "Yes, you can."

"That doesn't mean David won't be helping me in the kitchen," Mrs. Bauer argued.

"It means David is needed more on the farm than in the kitchen."

"But I need him, too. You said—"

David stopped listening. The Bauers were not the best of parents, but right now it was true that they needed him. He liked his room with its comfortable bed. He liked Mrs. Bauer's good cooking. And he liked farmwork. He'd learn from the Bauers how to be a good farmer, and someday—maybe—he might even have a farm of his own.

During the next few days Mr. Bauer did most of Amos's work himself. David also pitched in, working so hard that each evening he almost fell asleep at supper. But he didn't mind. He liked knowing that he was helping to keep the farm running smoothly.

Then one evening after supper Mr. Bauer wiped his mouth with his napkin and cleared his throat. "It will soon be time for the harvest," he said. "I am going to hire some field hands. I will decide who to hire. I will not let the Klan tell me what to do."

David spoke up. "I'll help with the harvest, too," he said. "I'll work hard."

Mr. Bauer nodded. "You already are a hard worker, David. I'm pleased with what you are doing. But I'm also planning for the future. Soon after the harvest is over, school will begin, and you must go to school."

"School?" David grew excited.

"It's a good thing I realized that you needed spectacles," Mr. Bauer said with a wink.

"What do you mean, *you* realized David needed spectacles?" Mrs. Bauer said. "*I'm* the one who noticed right away that David would see better—even work better—if he had a pair of spectacles."

"Nonsense. As I remember—"

David swallowed his laughter and touched his spectacles. How he wished he could talk to Amos. He missed the days when they would work in the fields together and joke about smelly old buttermilk.

David hoped that wherever Amos was, he was fine and happy. And he longed to tell his chum Mickey that everything had turned out like he said it would. Maybe that night, after the stars came out, David would tell them. And maybe, as he watched the stars shining in the clear night sky, he would hear his friends talking back.

EPILOGUE

LETTER FROM DAVID HOWARD
TO FRANCES MARY KELLY

Dear Miss Kelly,

Since Mr. and Mrs. Bauer took me in I've learned a lot of things. How to milk cows and how to feed chickens and hogs and split kindling and peel potatoes. That's just part of what I do. I have a lot of chores, and as I get bigger and stronger I'm going to learn to do more of the heavy work. I've decided that when I grow up I'm going to be a farmer with a farm of my own.

Best of all, I did find a new friend, just like you said. His name is Amos. Ever since he gave me a pair of spectacles, I can see things I never saw before. Sometimes at night I look up at the stars, just like my chum Mickey told me. I can see them. And I know that Mickey and Amos are looking at the same stars, too.

Thank you for helping me find a home.

Your friend,

David Howard

Glossary

blacksmith ***blak′ smith*** A person who makes horseshoes and attaches them to horses' hooves.

churn ***churn*** A container in which cream is stirred to make butter.

farmhand ***farm′ hand*** A hired worker on a farm.

greenbacks ***grēn′ baks*** U.S. paper money, first issued in 1861. Named for the green color of the bills.

kindling ***kind′ ling*** Small sticks that burn easily, used to start fires.

miserly ***mī′ zer lē*** Stingy, not generous.

nightshirt ***nīt′ shurt*** A loose shirt that reaches to the knees; worn in bed.

nightstick ***nīt′ stik*** A heavy stick or club carried by a policeman.

plantation ***plan tā′ shun*** A large farm in a Southern state on which cotton or tobacco was grown.

pump ***pump*** A machine with a handle that is moved up and down to raise water from a well.

separator ***sep′ a rā ter*** A container that allows cream to rise to the top of milk and be skimmed off.

shod ***shod*** A horse is shod when metal horseshoes have been fastened to its hooves.

slop ***slop*** Watery food for hogs.

spectacles ***spek′ ta kuls*** Eyeglasses.

sponge cake ***sponge′ cake*** A light, sweet, yellow cake made with eggs.

stickpin ***stik′ pin*** A fancy pin that holds a necktie or scarf in place.

swells ***swells*** A slang term for rich people.

tack room ***tack′ room*** A room in a barn used to store saddles, harnesses, and other equipment (tack) for horses.

urchin ***ur′ chin*** A mischievous youngster.

The Story of the Orphan Trains

In 1850 there were five hundred thousand people living in New York City. Ten thousand of these people were homeless children.

Many of these children were immigrants—they had come to the United States with their families from other countries. Many lived in one-room apartments. These rooms had stoves for heating and cooking, but the only water was in troughs in the hallways. These apartments were called tenements, and they were often crowded together in neighborhoods.

Immigrant parents worked long hours for very low wages. Sometimes they had barely enough money to buy food. Everyone in the family over the age of ten was expected to work. Few of these children could attend school, and many could not read or write.

Girls took in bundles of cloth from clothing

New York City's Lower East Side during the late nineteenth century.
Courtesy the Children's Aid Society

manufacturers. They carefully sewed men's shirts, women's blouses, and babies' gowns. Or they made paper flowers and tried to sell them on the busy streets.

Boys shined shoes or sold newspapers.

There were no wonder medicines in the 1800s. Many immigrants who lived in poor conditions died from contagious diseases. Children often became orphans with no one to care for them.

Some orphaned children were taken in by aunts and uncles. But many of the immigrant children had no relatives to come to their aid. They had left their grandparents, aunts, and uncles in other countries. They were alone. No one in the government had developed any plans for caring for them.

These orphans were evicted from their homes so that the rooms could be rented to other families. Orphans with no homes and no beds slept in alleys.

This was a time in which children were expected to work hard, along with adults. They were expected to take care of themselves. But there were not enough jobs for all the orphans in New York

A New York City "street arab."
Courtesy the Children's Aid Society

City. Many street arabs, as they were called, turned to lives of crime.

Charles Loring Brace, a young minister and social worker, became aware of this situation. He worried about these children, who so badly needed care. With the help of some friends, he founded the Children's Aid Society. The Children's Aid Society provided a place to live for some of the homeless children. It also set up industrial schools to train the children of the very poor in job skills.

Charles Loring Brace soon realized, however, that these steps were not enough. He came up with the idea of giving homeless, orphaned children a second—and much better—chance at life by taking them out of the city and placing them in homes in rural areas of the country.

Brace hired a scout to visit some of the farm communities west of New York State. He asked the scout to find out if people would be interested in taking orphan children into their homes. The scout was surprised by how many people wanted the children.

One woman wrote, "Last year was a very hard

Charles Loring Brace, founder of the Children's Aid Society and the orphan train program.
Courtesy the Children's Aid Society

A boy proudly holds up his Children's Aid Society membership card.
Courtesy the Children's Aid Society

year, and we lost many of our children. Yes, we want your children. Please send your children."

Brace went to orphans who were living on the streets and told them what he wanted to do. Children flocked to the Children's Aid Society office. "Take me," they begged. "Please take me."

"Where do you live?" the children were asked.

The answer was always the same: "Don't live nowhere."

The first orphan train was sent west in 1856, and the last one in 1929. During these years more than a hundred and fifty thousand children were taken out of New York City by the Children's Aid Society. Another hundred thousand children were sent by train to new homes in the West by the New York Foundling Home. By 1929 states had established welfare laws and had begun taking care of people in need, so the orphan trains were discontinued.

Before a group of children was sent west by train, notices that the children were coming would be placed in the newspapers of towns along the route: "WANTED: HOMES FOR CHILDREN," one notice said. It then listed the Society's rules. Children were to be treated as members of the family. They were to be taken to church on Sundays and sent to school until they were fourteen.

Handbills were posted in the towns where the orphan train stopped, where people could easily see

Boys on board an orphan train.
Courtesy the Children's Aid Society

them. One said: "CHILDREN WITHOUT HOMES. A number of the Children brought from New York are still without homes. Friends from the country, please call and see them."

A committee of local citizens would be chosen at each of the towns. The members of the committee

TERMS ON WHICH BOYS ARE PLACED IN HOMES.

ALL APPLICANTS MUST BE ENDORSED BY THE COMMITTEE

Boys fifteen years old are expected to work till they are eighteen for their board and clothes. At the end of that time they are at liberty to make their own arrangements.

Boys between twelve and fifteen are expected to work for their board and clothes till they are eighteen, but must be sent to school a part of each year, after that it is expected that they receive wages.

Boys under twelve are expected to remain till they are eighteen, and must be treated by the applicants as one of their own children in matters of schooling, clothing and training.

Should a removal be necessary it can be arranged through the committee or by writing to the Agent.

The Society reserves the right of removing a boy at any time for just cause.

We desire to hear from every child twice a year.

All Expenses of Transportation are Paid by the Society.

CHILDREN'S AID SOCIETY.
24 ST. MARKS PLACE, N.Y.

E. TROTT, AGENT.

Families that wanted to adopt an orphan train rider had to follow rules such as these.
Courtesy the Children's Aid Society

were given the responsibility of making sure that the people who took the orphan train children in were good people.

Most committee members tried to do a good job. But sometimes a child was placed in a home that turned out to be unhappy. Some farmers wanted free labor and were unkind to the boys they chose. But there were many good people who wanted to provide loving homes for the orphans.

Many people were so happy with their children that they took a step beyond being foster parents and legally adopted them.

Not all the children who were taken west on the orphan trains were orphans. Some had one or both parents still living. But sometimes fathers and mothers brought their children to the Children's Aid Society.

"I can't take care of my children," they would say. "I want them to have a much better life than I can give them. Please take them west to a new home."

What did the orphan train children think about their new lives? What made the biggest impression on them? They were used to living in small spaces, surrounded by many people in a noisy, crowded city. Were they overwhelmed by the sight of miles of open countryside?

Many of them had never tasted an apple. How did they react when they saw red apples growing on trees?

When they sat down to a meal with their new

A group of children ready to board the orphan trains, and their placing-out agents.
Courtesy the Children's Aid Society

families, did they stuff themselves? And did they feel a little guilty, remembering the small portions of food their parents had to eat?

Were they afraid to approach the large farm animals? What was it like for them to milk a cow for the first time?

WHAT IS NEEDED

Money is needed to carry forward this great child-saving enterprise. With more confidence do we ask it, since it has been so clearly shown that this work of philanthropy is not a dead weight upon the community. Though its chief aim is to rescue the helpless child victims of our social errors, it also makes a distinct economic return in the reduction of the number of those who are hopeless charges upon the common purse. More money at our command means more power to extend this great opportunity of help to the many homeless children in the boys' and girls' lodging houses in New York, and in the asylums and institutions throughout the State. We therefore ask the public for a more liberal support of this noble charity, confident that every dollar invested will bring a double return in the best kind of help to the children, so pitifully in need of it.

TABLE SHOWING THE NUMBER OF CHILDREN AND POOR FAMILIES SENT TO EACH STATE

State	Number	State	Number
New York	33,053	North Dakota	975
New Jersey	4,977	South Dakota	43
Pennsylvania	2,679	Kentucky	212
Maryland	563	Georgia	317
Delaware	833	Tennessee	233
District of Columbia	172	Mississippi	210
Canada	566	Florida	600
Maine	43	Alabama	50
New Hampshire	136	North Carolina	144
Vermont	262	South Carolina	191
Rhode Island	340	Louisiana	70
Massachusetts	375	Indian Territory	59
Connecticut	1,588	Oklahoma	95
Ohio	7,272	Arkansas	136
Indiana	3,955	Montana	83
Illinois	9,172	Wyoming	19
Iowa	6,675	Colorado	1,563
Missouri	6,088	Utah	31
Nebraska	3,442	Idaho	52
Minnesota	3,258	Washington	231
Kansas	4,150	Nevada	59
Michigan	5,326	Oregon	90
Wisconsin	2,750	California	168
Virginia	1,634	New Mexico	1
West Virginia	149	Texas	1,527

This chart, from the Children's Aid Society's 1910 bulletin, shows the number of children who rode the orphan trains and the states to which they were sent.

Courtesy the Children's Aid Society

Three sisters who were taken in by the Children's Aid Society after their mother had died. At the time the photograph was taken, the two youngest girls had been adopted.
Courtesy the Children's Aid Society

During the first few years of the orphan trains, the records kept by the Children's Aid Society were not complete. In a later survey taken in 1917, the Children's Aid Society researched what had happened to many of the orphan train children who had grown up.

They found that among them were a governor of North Dakota, a governor of the Territory of Alaska, two members of the United States Congress, nine members of state legislatures, two district attorneys, two mayors, a justice of the Supreme Court, four judges, many college professors, teachers, journalists, bankers, doctors, attorneys, four army officers, and seven thousand soldiers and sailors.

Although there were some problems in this system of matching homeless children with foster parents, the orphan train program did what it set out to do. It gave the homeless children of New York City the chance to live much better lives.

The Children's Aid Society is still active today, helping more than 100,000 New York City children and their families each year. The Society's services include adoption and foster care, medical and dental care, counseling, preventive services, winter and summer camps, recreation, cultural enrichment, education, and job training.

For more information, contact:

The Children's Aid Society
105 East 22nd Street
New York, NY 10010

The Civil Rights Movement

Every citizen of the United States is entitled to certain rights that guarantee personal freedom. We call these civil rights. In reality, not all citizens of the United States have always been able to exercise these rights. African Americans in the United States have had a particularly long and difficult struggle for civil rights.

When the Civil War ended in 1865, slavery was abolished and four million slaves were freed. The end of the war was followed by a period called the Reconstruction era. Reconstruction was meant to bring the Southern states back into the Union. It also led to new laws that gave civil rights—including the right to vote—to Southern blacks.

Unfortunately, the Reconstruction laws also led to the first appearance in the South of the Ku Klux Klan, a secret society made up of former Confederate soldiers. Klan members wore white robes, masks, and hoods and practiced strange rituals.

They believed that whites were better than blacks, and they terrorized blacks throughout the South. They beat and killed blacks and those whites who supported blacks' civil rights. The Ku Klux Klan has disappeared and reappeared in the South more than once and, sadly, is still active today.

Although they didn't always guarantee full rights to blacks, some important amendments to the Constitution and laws were passed that began the process. The Fourteenth Amendment, passed in 1867, said that a state could not take away the civil rights of any U.S. citizen. The Fifteenth Amendment, passed in 1868, said that no one could be denied the right to vote, regardless of race, color, or "previous condition of servitude"—that is, because he or she was once a slave.

In 1954 the Supreme Court made an important decision in the case of *Brown v. Board of Education of Topeka.* The Supreme Court stated that segregated schools—those schools that did not admit black students—were unconstitutional.

The Civil Rights Act of 1964 outlawed literacy

tests as a qualification for voting and banned all public segregation. This act also said it was unlawful for employers to base hiring decisions on a person's race, religion, or sex.

Even after these amendments and laws had been passed, most African Americans still could not vote because of loopholes in state laws. Finally the Voting Rights Act of 1965 outlawed all tests and taxes required to vote.

Probably the most important figure in the civil rights movement was Martin Luther King, Jr. King fought for equal rights for blacks and believed in working for social change through nonviolent protest. He supported Rosa Parks, a black woman who refused to sit at the back of a segregated bus, and he fought for black voting rights. He also led a historic protest march on Washington, D.C., during which he delivered his famous "I Have a Dream" speech. King won the Nobel Peace Prize in 1964 for his work. He was assassinated April 4, 1968, in Memphis.

After all this time, and thanks to leaders like Martin Luther King, Jr., African Americans today have full civil rights. Unfortunately, the Ku Klux Klan still exists, and racism remains an ugly fact of life. But today many African Americans hold public office in places where once they couldn't even vote.

SOURCES:

The Reader's Companion to American History, edited by Eric Foner and John A. Garraty, Boston: Houghton Mifflin Company, 1991

Stewart, Jaffrey C., *1001 Things Everyone Should Know about African American History.* New York: Doubleday, 1996.

About the Author

Joan Lowery Nixon is the acclaimed author of more than a hundred books for young readers. She has served as president of the Mystery Writers of America and as regional vice-president for the Southwest Chapter of that society. She is the only four-time winner of the Edgar Allan Poe Best Juvenile Mystery Award given by the Mystery Writers of America. She is also a two-time winner of the Golden Spur Award, which she won for *A Family Apart* and *In the Face of Danger,* the first and third books of the Orphan Train Adventures, which include *Caught in the Act, A Place to Belong, A Dangerous Promise, Keeping Secrets,* and *Circle of Love.* She was moved by the true experiences of the children on the nineteenth-century orphan trains to research and write the Orphan Train Adventures, as well as the Orphan Train Children books, which include *Lucy's Wish, Will's Choice, Aggie's Family,* and *David's Search.*

Joan Lowery Nixon and her husband live in Houston.